Lillian Hinman Shuey

California sunshine

Lillian Hinman Shuey

California sunshine

ISBN/EAN: 9783743463615

Manufactured in Europe, USA, Canada, Australia, Japa

Cover: Foto ©Andreas Hilbeck / pixelio.de

Manufactured and distributed by brebook publishing software
(www.brebook.com)

Lillian Hinman Shuey

California sunshine

CALIFRONIA · SUNSHINE.

VOICES OF THE YEAR.'

ON SAN JOAQUIN.

IN MEMORIAM.

MOODS.

CALIFORNIA SUNSHINE.

LILLIAN HINMAN SHUEY.

———

" He either fears his fate too much,
Or his deserts are small,
Who fears to put it to the touch,
To win or lose it all."
—*Marquis of Montrose.*

———

OAKLAND, CALIFORNIA.
PACIFIC PRESS PUBLISHING COMPANY.
MDCCCLXXXVIII.

"O flowering stretches glow and shine,
The language of my heart is thine. '

Dedicated to My First Love:

The Sacramento Grammar School Class of Sixty-nine.

CONTENTS.

—o—

VOICES OF THE YEAR.

—o—

Contents.

————o————

ON THE SAN JOAQUIN.

——o——

i

———O———

IN MEMORIAM.

——o——

———O———

MOODS.

——o——

VOICES OF THE YEAR.

CALIFORNIA.

Sown is the golden grain; planted the vines.
Fall swift, O loving rain. Lift prayers, O pines.
O green land, O gold land, fair land by the sea,
The trust of thy children reposes in thee.

(xi)

VOICES OF THE YEAR.

LIST the voices of the year!
   Softly, hear!
   Wandering near
Come their whispers to my ear;
   As they fleet,
Crowding thoughts their joys repeat.

April sings in cloudy air,
   So bright and fair,
   All unaware
That pearls are shimmering down her hair;
   While the sound
Seems like rain-drops strewn around.

Through the passion song of May
   Sweet hopes stray,
   Such as play
O'er young hearts unwrought to pray,
   Gladdening still
Lovers on the flowered hill.

Hark! the wild dove's plaintive tune;
   It is June.
   Far too soon

Reapers love the rest of noon.
　　The flowers die
All weary of the wide, hot sky.

Hear the rustling through the wheat!
　　Words complete—
　　Praises sweet—
Made the harvest wealth to greet,
　　While the days
Golden in the summer haze.

Now the tones of summer pale,
　　Fade and fail—
Hist! the quail
Whistling on the mountain trail;
　　Softly, hush,
Hunters in the underbrush.

Voices in a monotone
　　Seem to moan.
　　Dry and lone
Are the pathways we have known.
　　Falling leaves
Flutter on the wingéd breeze.

Windy voices, faint and fine,
　　Weave in rhyme,
　　As ye chime

Hopes and fears of seeding-time,
    When each grain,
List'ning, waits the sound of rain.

—§—

THE CHARIOTS OF HEAVEN.

BREAK forth into chorus of singing,
    Ye silver-tongued birds of the sky,
For the South Wind, the South Wind is bringing
    His horsemen and chariots by.

The horsemen and hosts of the conqueror,
    The king and his cohorts of rain,
See, see, how the legions sweep over
    The land of the vine and the grain!

Drought and his minions are vanquished,
    The conqueror's raiment is kissed;
And the spirits of famine and sorrow
    Went out in the shroud of the mist.

Far roll the gray chariots of heaven;
    The mountains allegiance bring.
The lowlands with emerald banners
    Proclaim that the South Wind is king.

Spring upward, spring upward, gold flowers,
  Bird choirs innumerable, sing!
For the hosts and the chariots have brought us
  The growth and the gladness of spring.

—§—

ROBERT, MY ROVER.

O ROBERT, my rover, the dew's on the clover
  And shining like pearls on the grain;
The lark and the linnet sing sweet every minute,
  A-wooing their loves in the lane.

The dry time is over, and rain through the clover
  Runs eastward in murmuring rills;
Thick grasses are growing, bright flowers are blowing,
  All over the hay-slopes and hills.

O Robert, my rover, how sweet is the clover
  Down there in the beautiful hay,
Where loitered we grieving, that night you were
    leaving
  To seek for your fortune away.

Now, Robert, my rover, the dry time is over,
  Sweet hope in our hearts may have room,
Like the perfuméd whiteness, the pink-tinted bright-
    ness,
  The glow of the orchard in bloom.

Soon blossoms the clover, then, Robert, my rover,
 The barley will shine like the sea;
Come back to the plowing, the haying, and Maying,
 Come home to the country and me.

—§—

APRIL, FAIR ENCHANTRESS.

SHE is so bright and winning,
 She is so fair and sweet,
She bids me not go sorrowing,
 She will not let me weep.

She flits before my windows,
 She tarries at my door,
And whispers to me softly,
 Oh, nourish care no more!

All day her voices call me,
 Bird airs and roundelays,
To leave life's mournful music,
 And sing unto her praise.

And when I wander sadly,
 As if to check my sighs
She spreads her nodding flowers
 Before my downcast eyes.

2

I draw my bonnet lower
   To hide her witching grace;
A merry breeze a-jesting
   Quick blows it from my face.

She warms my cheeks with kisses,
   She snatches every tear;
She lifts my soul with beauty,
   She calms each trembling fear.

Soft, fleecy clouds go dreaming
   Across the heavenly blue;
Wide stretch the emerald meadows,
   All cool with morning dew.

She is my gay enchantress,
   My April rare and sweet;
She bids me not go sorrowing,
   She will not let me weep.

——§——

MY GIRL.

WAS Sierra so proud of its forests,
   Or crown of its pearl,
Was a miser so rich in his treasure,
   As I in my girl?

Was ever a mother so blessed
　And happy as I?
My girl is a gem to my life,
　As stars to the sky.

She is lying at rest on my bosom,
　A flower asleep.
God grant that her blue eyes may open,
　Yet never to weep.

I pray that no anguish may furrow
　The brow of my girl,
Nor that sad years of sorrow may silver
　This delicate curl.

If thus should God grant to my darling
　A life without pain,
He would close these dear eyes to the sunshine,
　Nor open again.

God knows that to live she must suffer
　And wander astray,
But he missions the angels to keep her
　The long weary way.

Safe be the path that they walk in,
　These little white feet,
May they grow into strength and perfection
　If rough ways they meet.

May charity flow from these fingers
　　Now folded at rest,
May they weave in life's wonderful fabric
　　Threads finest and best.

A heart all untried has my darling,
　　A pure heart I know;
God grant that earth's brave ones will help her
　　In keeping it so.

And thus at the shrine of my treasure
　　I wait with a prayer;
While my hopes go out to the future—
　　For my answer is there.

—§—

BERKELEY BLOSSOMS.

BERKELEY blossoms bright and rare,
Sweetest blossomed anywhere,
　　Were ye mindful of your duties,
　　While the sunlight died your beauties,
As ye budded slow and saintly in the summer air?

Berkeley roses, gold and cream,
Did your folded petals dream
　　Most of dark, sad rooms, and faces

Turning mutely to the vases
Where your bending clusters would in stately beauty
 gleam ?

Did ye dream so, cream and white,
Waxen roses, frail and light,
 Of the pain ye would dissemble,
 Of the fingers that would tremble
To reach forth and clasp you in the weary wakeful
 night?

Purple pansies, widely blown,
In your fancies was it known
 What your mistress was desiring,
 Bending o'er you so—untiring,
While her soul's sweet musings in her clear eyes
 shone ?

Heliotrope, in bud and bloom,
Breathing fragrance to the noon,
 She had meanings rare and tender,
 She had duties for your splendor,
As she cut and bound you for the sorrow-haunted
 room.

Dewy, dainty, softly fair,
Berkeley blossoms ye were there,
 In the gilded vases smiling,
 All the long sad hours beguiling,
While about you hovered, seemly, lost words from a
 prayer.

California Sunshine.

MAY, 1883.

———

MAY, thou art come at last,
The reign of clouds is past;
No more the chilling wind
So rude will be, unkind,
And shut me in all day,
Thou'rt come at last, sweet May.

I've looked for you before,
And opened blind and door,
That I might speak you fair,
But March stood frowning there.
But now once more, sweet May,
Your smile has blessed the day.

I love your gentle air,
Your shadows warm and fair,
Your pale, soft, distant skies,
Your tree-top melodies.
And all the cloudless day
My thought is yours, sweet May.

O May, go not too soon,
Close on the skirts of June,
You came with tardy feet,
So transient and so fleet
Will be your glad bright stay,
I pray you wait, sweet May.

O linnet singing so,
And May, you cannot know
What peace your charms impart;
Heart songs to being start, .   .
And care is driven away
By thy return, sweet May.

——§——

A DECEMBER WALK.

A BARREN field, a treeless plain;
    A landscape growing green;
A hueless sky, a distant cry—
    A lifeless, voiceless scene.

A pebble path on fallow soil;
    A step of noiseless fall;
A stone, a clod, the starting grass,
    A dampness over all.

No blossoms, daisy-eyed, appear,
    No songs of summer pass;
A kill-deer, lone, brown-throated, glides,
    Seeking the tender grass.

All nature sleeps, to dream, perchance,
    In visions bright and sweet,
What time the restive lover, Spring,
    Will amorous tales repeat.

Then will her heart responsive thrill,
  And, waking from her rest,
Love's magic words will make replies
  In blossoms on her breast.

——§——

LAW ·VERSUS· JUSTICE.

A SATIRE.

SWEET Justice walking out one day,
  A miss of lovely carriage,
Was met by Law, who loved straightway,
  And asked her hand in marriage.

She gave assent and with him strayed
  Through many a lover's bower,
Till once he said, " My pretty maid,
  How much will be your dower?"

Fair Justice dropped her shining eyes,
  And trembled with emotion,
And said, " Just love, my noble sir,
  And thanks will be my portion."

" I could not eat such stuff," he cried,
  His hand in parting giving,
" And with my hands unto you tied,
  How could I make a living?"

Forever shrinking in the woods
Does stricken Justice tarry,
And never while the world goes round
Will Law and Justice marry.

———§———

SEPTEMBER DAYS.

I LIKE these low, calm days,
These far, pale reaches, and the autumn haze,
That o'er the distant fields comes low and near
To shield the fading glories of the year.

All nature lies at rest,
And labor's tumult, surging from her breast,
Has swept away the stifling breath of care;
A peaceful stillness dreams upon the air.

There is a calm content,
The summer's wearing eagerness is spent.
May not ambition too forsake her ways
And court the drowsy genius of the days?

The river's tide is low;
No tender grasses by the high banks grow.
The birds are silent in the shadows deep,
And all the flowers have hid away in sleep.

But there are forces still;
The dusty whirlwind mounts the yellow hill;
Uncertain gusts of wind sweep here and there,
While misty powers rule the upper air.

· We well may wait and rest,
The zest of life but slumbers in the breast;
Strength will return, and shining hope impart
A force and courage to the wakened heart.

——§——

IN THE BARLEY FIELD.

ALL down the dewy barley
    The morning calls me near,
And sweetening every moment, .
    The linnet's song I hear.
The light is pure and silvery,
    The warm-souled poppy blows;
And rich about my pathway
    The dewy barley grows.

All down the distant meadow,
    In stately, jeweled rows, .
Ten thousand banners herald
    The softest wind that blows;
The light is pure and silvery,
    The high mist sweeps away,

The lark with crystal changes
  Keeps ringing up the day.

Far down the dreamy meadow
  I tread the tender grass,
And breathe the broken fragrance
  Exhaling as I pass.
The air is pure and silvery,
  A mirror bright and still,
Where shine the flowered reaches
  Across the clear-cut hill.

All in the emerald barley,
  Where pearls were thickly strewn,
The morning hides her jewels
  Before the glance of noon.
The light grows warm and golden;
  In cool, luxuriant rows,
Where wait the tired songsters,
  The dewy barley grows.

—§—

CLAYTON.
CONTRA COSTA COUNTY.

FAIR emerald town! a jewel placed
  Within such setting rare!
How soft thy upland breezes sweep!
  How sweet thy crystal air!

The ancient mountain loved thee well,
  And gave for thy repose
His fairest vale, where grows the pine,
  And blooms the mountain rose.

Dear highland village, nestled down
  Beneath the mountain's heart,
Thy cherished shades are lovelier far
  Than muffled aisles of art.

And ne'er upon thy beauteous form
  The chilling snow-clouds fall;
The myrtle's bloom, the violet's breath,
  Come ever at thy call.

Thou hast no changes, heavenly places,
  No melancholy hours,
For spring has claimed thee for her own
  And wreathed thy year with flowers.

——§——

BIRD OF ART.

A LITTLE singing bird of art
From printed page took sudden start
  And nestled in my breast.
A thoughtful verse of tuneful rhyme,

A gentle chant, in perfect time,
  A melody of rest.

A little rhythmic bird of art
Escaped from some high-crownèd heart,
  A pearl-winged, singing dove.
It brought a message unto me,
In rhyme and time and symphony,
  And softly sang of love.

——§——

A CLEAR DAY IN WINTER.

———

THE lark, with song divine,
  Lifts up his praises to the winter morn
Because the golden sun once more doth shine
  O'er grassy fields by windy torrents torn.

The sweet and calm sunlight
  Calls forth his triumph loud,
The while he cleaveth swift with new delight
  Some misty skirt of night-exhausted cloud.

He knows full well, poor lark,
  That clouds will roll amain,
To fling across the green their shadows dark
  And flood the brimming pools with splashing rain.

Oh, linger long, bright day,
  That hope may cleave the dark
And glorify the paths all dull and gray
  Where once my soul went singing like the lark.

——§——

THE SUMMER.

THE summer wore away,
And yet we idled on the tented green,
Or boated inland on the peaceful stream,
  Divining, day by day,
Th' unfolding beauties of the mingled scene.

——§——

A MOUNTAIN SPRING.

I KNEEL, as kneels before a shrine a soul
All worn and burdened with such sins as roll
Deep torture to the heart, and troubled so
Before the Immanuel fountain boweth low.
How gray my garments with the dust!　My feet
How burned and weary with the wayside heat!
With dust upon my brow I cry, "Unclean,"
And lave my heated hands beneath the stream;
A mountain spring, cool-crystaled to the brink,

And flinging jets of diamonds as I drink,
And circled round by green, wide-polished leaves.
With low-boughed hazels and tall cedar trees,

An altar perfected in nature's love
By unsealed fountains from the heights above,
The music of the place in sacred tones,
Soft measures keep upon the granite stones;
Calm, holy symphonies to being start,
And make sweet pleading to my weary heart.
The water, shade, the scarlet flowers that blow,
Bright shafts of gladness to my being throw;
I rise baptized with coolness and with rest,
And pluck the scarlet blossoms for my breast.

—§—

WHY SING OF YOUTH.

WHY do ye sing of youth?
Such times were sweet in truth,
  But why go singing all the working day
For what will not return?
Those loves for which ye yearn
  Will never from their dusky pathway stray.

In vain to call and sigh,
For they will ne'er reply
  Who underneath the grass or marble sleep;

And some who love you not,
Your very name forgot,
  They would not listen, could they hear you weep.

All through the shining spring,
When birds, rejoicing, sing,
  I hear ye singing in your hedgèd lane
For golden-tinted dreams,
For those old ways and scenes,
  While memory's tears are falling as the rain.

Dear friends, my power is weak
To touch your heart or speak
  Of all the sweet, bright things that crowd your way
E'en though your nerve powers fail
E'en though your brow is pale
  And over-hung with locks of silver grey.

Dost hear the lark sing loud?
Dost see that gilt-edged cloud?
  Dost feel the breath of spring upon your cheek?
Dost love no more the stars
In rank-like golden bars,
  That something of the Heaven beyond bespeak?

And love is not gone by;
There's many reaching high
  To win your heart or clasp your quiet hand.
You cannot be too old
To rescue from the cold
  Some weary one, wave-driven from the strand.

Why, what is every year
Which you so sadly fear,
   But one more harvest, bearing sheaves of truth?
For all the gold of age,
For wisdom's precious page,
   What could you take from festive, giddy youth?

There is a calm content,
There is a fever spent,
   Mad passion neath the hand of peace is mute.
Why sing of youth at all,
When leaves about us fall,
   Down dropping from the laden boughs of fruit?

CLOUDS OF APRIL.

APRIL showers floating by,
Bank on bank of clouds rolled high,
Let your hurried masses lower,
Thirsty fields your love implore,
Leaves and blossoms bid you come,
April clouds, no longer roam.

Heavy hosts with silver wings,
Anxious thought your fleeting brings,
Beauteous clouds, why eastward speed?
Tarry to our waiting need.
Come, o'er-weep us, clouds above,
Low encircle us with love.

Let us feel your throbbing heart;
Passion's fullness o'er us part.
Earth invites you to her breast,
Clouds, wind-blown across the west;
April showers, pass not all,
Let your benedictions fall.

——§——

THE LILY CUP.

[Written for Donna Winning.]
'TWAS a child's face there upturned,
With a purity unharmed;
   Eyes, Madonna-like and fair,
Such as bore unto me faintly
Thoughts of faces "shrinéd saintly"
   In the sayings of a prayer.

'Twas a child's face sweetly wrought
Into lines of older thought;
   And its innocence and grace
Bade me tarry from the thronging,
Bowed me with a tender longing—
   Made an altar of the place.

Sinless lips were pressed to mine
At this holy wayside shrine;
   Then more swiftly sped my feet,

For this child-face looking up
Like a pure-leaved lily-cup,
 Had rebuked my heart's deceit.

——§——

ARBOR DAY.

O YE hills, scarred with mines, desolated!
 O ye vast, shadeless valleys of wheat!
Hear ye the great words of the poet?
 Western winds, speed away, and repeat,

To the bared, wasted slopes of Sierra,
 " Ye shall yet in your childen be blessed,
For the signals of hope will be lifted
 On the mist-laden hills of the West."

Arbor day! arbor day! God be with us!
 I see the green banners draw near,
And the rivers long hid in the mountains
 In their old stony pathways appear.

Arbor day in the old El Dorados!
 Whose birthright of beauty was sold
When the forests that leaned to the rivers
 Made way for the triumphs of gold.

Arbor day in the wide rolling valleys!
 Where the rivers run silent and deep;

Where the sway of the conquering plowshare,
  The grove and the hedge-row will keep.

Arbor day on the hills looking seaward !
  Arbor day by the shimmering bay,
And the forest-bound heights by the ocean
  The breath of the tempest will stay.

Arbor day for the land of my childhood !
  Let the child arms their offerings lend.
For down the green paths of the future
  I see the fair children descend.

Shout aloud, all ye long, barren ridges !
  Sing for joy, oh, my desolate plain!
'Tis the chant of the South Wind proclaiming
  The coming and love of the rain.

---§---

MY SOUTH WIND.

STEADILY blow, my Wind, steadily, oh,
  Faithfully, faithfully blow,
Up with a will to the mountain so still,
  Over the meadows below.

My South Wind late, thy speeding we wait,
  And the high-piled clouds you keep

Marshaled afar where the Rain Kings are,
　　Away on the measureless deep.

Oh, proud and strong, like an ocean song,
　　Steadily, haughtily blow;
And over the air now mute with a prayer,
　　An anthem of raining throw.

My South Wind brave, speed up from the wave
　　Each weary and passionate cloud,
To weep out its pain on thy breast with rain,
　　My comforter, crowned and proud.

My Ruler, my King, come in triumph and bring
　　The hope of your heart, my love,
Chanting the strain of the on-coming rain
　　Borne on thy pinions above.

—§—

A DECEMBER DAY.

When the morning mists are rising,
　　And the fog has cleared away,
Over all the emerald meadows
　　Comes my clear and perfect day.
Oh, the dawning of the sunbeams
　　Through the thin and breaking mist !

Oh, the lifting of the mountains,
　By the golden heralds kissed.

Goes the pure and gentle morning,
　Azure-robed and crystal-crowned,
While the jewels in the grasses
　Hedge her queenly progress round;
Hedge and hold her, brightly fold her,
　As she slowly fades away,
Then again in grassy shadows
　Hide before the amorous day.

Wide and clear the noon-time groweth,
　Songless birds on grey wings pass,
While the soul of singing Spring-time,
　Waits and listens in the grass;
Waits and listens for the chiming
　Of the bells beyond the blue,
For they only know the passing
　Of the Old Year into New.

Nay, 'tis not the bleak December;
　'Tis a green and growing clime,
And the Angel of the seasons
　Keeps the passing of the time.
Smiling brightly he has written,
　In the book of seasons told,
In the golden West the New Year
　Is no gladder than the Old.

A PEAR TREE ON AUBURN RAVINE.

PRIDE of the morning! Joy of the sun!
Regal-crowned, magnificent one!
Burdened with odorous bloom, and bright
As a bride in her shimmering jewels of light,
Thou wilt gladden the sun-burnished noon,
My radiant pear tree abloom.

Proud is the wayside! Rare is the day
Where thou stand'st in thy snow-white array;
Skylarks with quivering breasts take wing,
All their triumph and joy on thy high boughs to sing,
Branches with wing-weary bees all atune,
My radiant pear tree abloom.

Winged with new promises, Angel of Spring,
All the hills their allegiance bring,
Burdened with bloom—so be burdened, bright tree,
With the hope and the trust that awaiteth on thee—
Thou the bride, all the valley the groom,
My radiant pear tree abloom.

—§—

THE GOLDEN SPIKE.

[Read before the Oregon State Grange.]
BRING here the golden spike!
The sunny empires by the Western sea
Shall drive the bolt that seals their unity.

The far Northwest draws near,
The distant South is here,
The white Cascades look down
To busy field and town;
The harvest-field is white!
The sounding rails unite!
The pulse of commere struggles to be free
Above the golden spike.

Bring here the golden spike!
Let North and South clasp hands, turn face to
        face,
Their new-born star of destiny to trace.
        Great deeds to action start,
        Strength moves from heart to heart,
        The quickened blood transfused
        Finds channels all unused,
        And weakness leaps to might;
        Drive here the golden spike
That frees the giant struggling in his place,
        With new-found worlds in sight.

The golden spike is in;
The driving steam is waiting for command;
The lofty mountains with their forests stand;
        The quarries yield their store,
        The mines their glittering ore,
        The lands of golden grain,
        The lands of summer rain,

Bright as eternal spring,
Their teeming harvests bring
Unto the rugged servant of the land—
The iron-sceptered king.

New worlds to prove in sight!
Clasp hands, and forward is the watchward now;
Forward the armies of the conquering plow;
For victory over death,
Over the dry wind's breath,
Over all things that hold
The earth from its hundred-fold.
Over dearth and blight,   ·
The hoar-frost in the night;
Forward the plow, that turns the desert wild
To garden places, where the prattling child
Is herald of God's might.

Bring here the golden spike!
The sunny empires by the Western sea
Shall know the bond that seals their unity;
The faith of mind in mind,
The trust of human kind,
The laws of brotherhood,   ·
All bonds for human good,
The golden rule, bedight
With heavenly love and light;
Thy willful deed, thy neighbor's deed shall be;
This is the golden spike!

There is a golden spike
Joining the nobler lines of human thought,
Whereby the best by feebler need is sought.
    The highest culture proves,
    The power of mind to move
    Beyond old lines.   God's will
    Is change and action still.
    If Justice, Love, and Right
    Their powerful bonds unite,
What iron ways of progress shall be wrought,
    Joined with the golden spike.

    Set here the golden spike—
    Whereby all men in equal glory stand;
Whereby great thoughts shall move across the
       land.
    Let Christian thought be freed
    Its sun-bright life to lead.
    Turn face, great Oregon,
    Give golden grace for grace,
    With new-found worlds in sight,
    For God, and home, and right,
To California give your warm, strong hand,
    And drive the " Golden Spike."

 ON SAN JOAQUIN.

ON SAN JOAQUIN.

On San Joaquin! on San Joaquin!
How rolls the tide of living green!
How sweeps the wind through billowy grain!
How falls the warm, life-giving rain!

O San Joaquin, so wide and free,
How swells thy distance like the sea!
Soft winds that love thee speed away
Far o'er the immeasurable realm of day.

O gentle skies so blue above,
The valley of my liel and love,
Thou'rt ever fair, though burnished clear,
Or hung with rain clouds drooping near.

On thy horizon far and fine,
The mountains stand in dim outline,
Whence rivers slow descend to keep
Their long, strong currents to the deep.

Oh, toss thy billows, San Joaquin,
Thy lifted waves of sunlit green!
Oh, flowering stretches glow and shine,
The homage of my heart is thine.

I know how sweet thy mornings rise,
Uplifted to the kindling skies,
With misty veil all fresh and fair
Entangling bird songs in the air.

I know how calm thy night looks down,
Clear-visioned in her radiant crown,
Whose moonlight all the distance fills,
And trails the far-off Western hills.

The swaying vine, the rustling grain,
The blossoming trees spread down the plain,
The bright alfalfa rolls between
Its fragrant meads of evergreen.

On San Joaquin! on San Joaquin!
The world thy beauteous tides has seen.
The circling years will bring to thee
A famed and glorious destiny.

—§—

MOURNING DOVE.

BIRD of sad tone,
Smoothing thy purple breast
And cooing such unrest
To slumberous June,

The faintest breath
Of violets hasteth by,
And on thy tremulous sigh
    Fades unto death.

A quick-turned head,
A breast but swelling so
As if its burdened woe
    Could ne'er be said,

Plain mourning bird,
It is not all thine own
The pain of this sad tone,
    So plaintive heard.

Some human heart,
Stricken beyond its due,
Bequeathed such fate to you,
    To mourn apart.

I ask of thee,
Sweet mourning dove, a boon,
To pale, thought-saddened June,
    Give sigh for me.

—§—

THE CROSS ON THE ROCK.
MARSH CAÑON.

I KNOW a vale where clouds of grey
O'er hay-bound hill-tops idly stray,

And shadows from each rocky steep
In long, cool grasses idly creep.

Here morning hears her latest call,
Here first the steps of evening fall,
Here noon, leaf-shadowed, glimmers down,
O'er wind-swept ridges high and brown;

Here stand those sturdy oaken trees,
Loud rustling to the gusty breeze,
Their old gnarled branches lifted high,
The pioneers of days gone by.

A crystal stream from blue hills led,
Goes rippling in its gravelly bed,
The sky, the bridge, the willows green,
All mirrored in its peaceful stream.

Above this vale where shadows lie
All day between the earth and sky,
A jutting rock, seam-lined and grey,
O'erlooks the tranquil, silent day.

And high upon its moss-stained wall,
Where flickering shadows on it fall,
There lies a cross carved true and deep,
Bright signet of the ancient steep.

What brave, heroic, long-lost deeds,
What sunken grave beneath the weeds,

Hath record in this carving old
Upon this rock nowhere is told.

The hand that carved it now is dust,
The steel long since was given to rust;
But time's swift sorrows are not thine,
Sweet altar of the wildwood shrine.

And this we know, no church reared high
Lifts holier anthems to the sky,
Than this deep vale where clouds sweep low,
And chanting winds through green aisles blow.

—§—

FOR FRIENDS.

I GIVE great thanks for each fair gift
  That grace or beauty lends
Unto the pathway of my life,
  But most of all for friends.

I will give thanks, this Day of Thanks,
  For sunshine, home, and health,
For love of all things pure and fair,
  For nature's beauteous wealth.

But most of all for friends, dear Lord,
  Whose honest hands I take;

Who give me trust, who keep my trust,
　Nor kind allegiance break ;

Who, through my goings out and in,
　Mute trustfulness outreach;
Nor give their faith for etiquette
　Or vagaries of speech;

Whose hearts are mine unfaltering,
　Whose doors would open wide
Should hopes and health and competence
　Be banished from my side.

My friends, here's thanks, this Day of Thanks,
　And here's my hand in token,
And never, while we pray God's grace,
　May hostile words be spoken.
Thanksgiving-day, 1882.

———§———

THE FLOATING COBWEBS OF SAN JOA-QUIN.

COBWEBS, drifting, drifting,
From the east land shifting,
　Drifting far as human eye can see,
In these silken gildings
What may be your tidings,
　What may be your message unto me ?

Going, ever going,
Throwing, slowly throwing,
  Slender silver threads from field to town.
On the dry weeds resting,
Many breezes breasting,
  Are the fairies weaving earth a gown?

Floating, onward floating,
O'er the damp clods gloating,
  From each standing straw in cables hung,
Forming phantom bridges
From the ruts and ridges,
  Shining bright and silvery in the sun.

Filmy fairy, spinning,
On your downy winging,
  Lightly, softly, touch my upheld hands;
From your silken gildings,
Tell to me your tidings,
  Any mysteries from unknown lands.

Cobwebs, floating, fleeting,
You have wound my feet in,
  From your lines I cannot make me free;
May be there's a letter
In your silken fetter,
  He, perchance, will telegraph to me.

Silken wires a-glistening, ·
As I wait a-listening,
   At these lines spread shining o'er the plain,
I will make a guessing
That this cobweb meshing
   Means the coming of a winter rain.

These the welcome tidings
In these silken gildings,
   Soon the skies their gentle gifts will yield,
With a dripping raining,
With a sweet refraining
   Of showers bending o'er the fallow field.

—§—

THE SPRING STORM ON THE SAN JOAQUIN.

THE warning thunder leads along the plain,
   And falls the rain in floods,
Laying against the ground the swaths of grain;
   Veiling the hills and yon slow-creeping train.

The flooded earth drinks water everywhere;
   The birds their coverts seek,
Leaving their singing places, beaten there
   By the wind sweeping along the heavy air.

We thought to hear no more the sound of rain,
  The storm wind raging wild,
And splashing showers flung against the pane;
  But now, to our distrust, descends the rain.

It beats upon the roof so brown and old,
  The eaves run trickling streams;
It sinks away into the upturned mould.
In wind, and rain, and warmth, God's gifts unfold.

—§—

SEEDING-TIME.

UNDER the showers of grain that fall,
Scattered about on the fallow soil,
Groweth the grain for the farmer's hand,
Lieth the hope of the furrowed land,
Falleth the steps of an unseen fate—
Fortune or failure lieth in wait.

Whir, whir, whir, goes the sowing machine,
Each grain drops to its place unseen.
Is the mother earth in a loving mood?
Will she give to each stray seed its food?
Will it ever lack for warmth or love,
Till its heavy head gives thanks above?

Under the promise the earth grows green;
Seed-time and harvest shall e'er be seen.

The dove went forth on its mission sent,
Led by the bow o'er the waters bent,
The promise of God came down on earth,
As the faith and food of man took birth.

Ready and steady old Tom and Dick
Pull on, till the seed grain lieth thick;
The squirrel chirps from his hilly row,
The wild geese flying circle low,
The blackbirds chattering fly again.
Hunger is not in the land of grain.

Pattering, pattering like the rain,
Falleth the showers of golden grain;
The farmer thinks of the weeds and rain
And a face that looks from the window-pane.
Oh, many a dream and many a need
Lies in the showers of falling seed.

—§—

AFTER DARK ON SAN JOAQUIN.

"Cookoo, cookoo," sweet bird,
Out in the barren grain-fields heard,
I wonder who are you,
In modulations sweet and true,
Thus calling through the dark, "Cookoo."

Where is your lonely nest?
What thought is trembling in your breast?
What color is the throat
That gives to night the distant note,
Like love to silence broke?

" Cookoo, cookoo," so near,
Hast summoned any sweetheart dear?
I wonder who you are,
Lone, plaintive, like a wandering star,
" Cookoo," so near, so far.

" Cookoo," my brave unknown;
The fields are wide and dry and lone,
There's dark and wind and dew,
The high faint starlight struggling through;
Yet still sounds sweet, " Cookoo."

" Cookoo, cookoo," I hear,
Borne through the silent air, so clear.
My heart has lost its pain
Thus listening to the calm refrain,
" Cookoo, cookoo," again.

——§——

THE OLD, OLD HOUSE.

Oh, 'tis an old brown house
Alone with the wind and dust;

Leaves are adrift on the porch,
  The lock, it is locked with rust.

We will enter the old, old house,
  Press open the creaking door;
Hollow echoes the tread
  Of steps on the dusty floor.

The bat, disturbed as we enter,
  Flies from his darkened domain;
The rat is prince of the corners,
  The spider, king of the pane.

We will live in the old, old house,
  Drive out the silence and gloom,
And the sounds of our life and mirth
  Will echo from room to room.

A pledge to the old, old house,
  Banish its gloom and decay,
And under its time-worn beams
  Welcome the joys of to-day.

We will lighten with color and cheer
  Its windows, doorways, and halls;
The pictures we hallow most dear
  Will smile from the brightened walls.

Oh, come to the old, old house,
   New hope will light up our eyes!
We will strive as we furnish and gild
   To take a new lease on our lives.

Let us call up the hopes and joys
   We cherished in other years;
We will shut from the house the gloom,
   Shut from our prospects the fears.

'Tis only an old, brown house,
   We'll crowd it with love-life bright,
And the courage that comes with faith
   Each sorrowing heart will light.

———§———

GOD FORGIVES.

WHAT if tears from trembling lids
   Burning fall upon the cheek ?
What if lips with sorrow sealed
   Broken words forego to speak?
What if harsh words sting the heart ?
   What if lives regret to live
For the darkness born therein ?
   It behooves us to forgive,
     God forgives.

What if dearest hopes are strewn
  By the careless hand of one?
What if sorrow's seeds are sown,
  Springing cherished buds among?
Ah, the sighs we cannot speak!
  Ah, the blows we dare not grieve!
Ah, the wrongs we fear to weep!
  It behooves us to forgive,
    God forgives.

Who does God forgive? Ah, me!
  Many a sin of word and deed,
Many a vain, ungrateful prayer,
  Many a base, unholy need.
What a debt hath God forgiven!
  What dumb prayers he will receive!
And for love of Him who loves,
  It behooves us to forgive,
    God forgives.

—§—

CHARACTER.

BUILD up thy pyramid higher,
Each step thou shalt build up entire
Will show to thy truth-seeking eyes
Life's broader horizons and skies.

WORKING FAITH.

A BIRD with a crimson-hued breast,
Up in the eaves in a place
Exposed, uncertain, unsafe,
Is constructing with patience his nest.

I have watched it with trembling and fear,
Lest the wind and storm would rend
And tear from my beautiful friend
All the work and the hope of the year;

But the bird has no fear of his own,
He twitters without and within,
He evermore tarries to sing
As he carries the twigs for his home.

He has taught me a beautiful creed.
Strength I would gather anew,
I would be caroling too,
If I trusted in God for each need

To this April-day lesson I bow,
Away with a doubt or a fear,
Away with the sigh and the tear,
Working trust is sufficient for now.

Do not gloomily, moodily say,
Be downcast, be anxious, be sad,
We should be hopeful and glad,
We should laugh, we should sing, we should pray.

THREE SISTERS.

THREE sisters came and gave their hands to me;
First April, changeful sprite of gaiety,
Then May, with hasting steps and riper bloom,
.Led softly in her rare, pale sister June.

And each brought gifts my welcoming to meet;
First April flung her jewels at my feet;
May, smiling, spread her gold-edged clouds above,
But June, divinest of the three, brought love.

To April, many a careless jest I tossed;
I gave to May the blossoms that I lost,
But unto June, beneath the oaken tree,
I gave the sacred thoughts of reverie.

—§—

WE ARE TOO PROUD.

WE are too proud, alas!
When tears fall fast,
On friendship's lap to rest our fevered cheeks;
With sad, averted eyes,
We fly when griefs arise,
Where solitude her chilly presence keeps.

The morn is fair, is sweet;
"Good-day," we most repeat;

Good day, good day to us and all our friends.
    If they but speak us fair,
    We have no need or care
What keen-armed agony each inner temple rends.

    O'er deep, great woes untold,
    We drop the silent fold
Of courtesy, or reticence, or pride;
    We smile into each face,
    And strive with charming grace
To win some whilom friend unto our side.

    Oh, helpless heart of men,
    How little do ye ken
What golden fruit a little trust might bear!
    Alas! we are too proud
    Our selfish wants to crowd,
Or ask of passing friends a pitying care.

—§—

THE LARK'S SONG.

O LARK! why do you sing such full, glad song
This winter morn? Such trills to spring belong.
The clouds ride fast along the gloomy sky,
The wind in misty gusts is speeding by;
Because the morn a few pale beams did bring
You sit and chant with bursting throat of spring.

There is no warmth or flowers or springing grain;
You are too forward with your gay refrain.
My thoughts are heavy, like the clouds to-day,
So plume yourself, brown bird, and dart away.

But still he sings, and cuts his song out clear,
As if he tried my tuneless heart to cheer.
Would I could learn when mortal skies are dark
To chant such crystal, ringing songs, O lark!

––—§—––

THE OLD MAN OF THE MOUNTAIN.

[In Pine Cañon, Mt. Diablo, there is a pile of rock on the summit of
a high cliff bearing an exact resemblance to a bowed old man. It is
called the "Mountain Builder."]

WHAT are you doing there, quaint old man,
There in the lead of the rocky van,
Half-covered, half-cloaked with the cold gray stone,
Keeping your watch in the mountains alone?

What are you thinking of, bent old sage,
Learnéd of years and crumbling with age?
What are you looking for there in the mould,
Waiting and watching on, careworn and old?

Oh! you are weary, sad, silent old man;
You sigh for the end of your life's long span.

Wild, ancient, and strange is the life you have led,
As the ages rolled over your grey, bowed head.

Weary are you of your toil, old man,
Builder of mountains since earth began,
Till bound by the ocean and burdened by care,
Stone-browed and stone-armed, rested you there.

In earth is your form, of rock is your head,
Your visage is cold and moss-grown and dead,
But I ween in your breast is a heart beating warm,
Hoping and praying in sunshine and storm.

Think on us, pray for us, patient old man,
Hope for us, weep for our sins if you can.
Think of the earth throng, turbulent, worn,
Over life's misty, dark precipice borne.

Keep patient, old man, till your rock life shall end,
Till the trump from the skies shall the rock ridges rend,
When out from your prison your glad soul shall rise
And join with the sages and saints in the skies.

——§——

MY HERBARIUM.

I TOOK my book of faded flowers
    With leaflets crisp and torn,
And stems all dry and desolate,
    That once sweet bloom had borne.

I turned these pages, rustling soft
    With frail and sere decay.
Alas! from every spring-time friend
    Sweet life had passed away.

But while my fingers turned the leaves,
    My mind to visions bent,
And back to nature's hours of bloom
    My thoughts in perfume went.

I saw the dead to life returned,
    And spring its memories win.
My fancy saw them not as now,
    But what they once had been.

This rose was once a beauteous thing,
    This violet, once how fair!
The meadow once with rapture bore
    These flowerets swaying there.

Each cup and bell and daffodil
    A history doth tell
Of summer sun, and summer songs—
    The Master giveth well.

And every flower that lieth here,
    Though met by death so soon,
Has reigned among its dainty peers,
    And graced the court of June.

These lowly herbs a lesson teach—
    That life is short and gay;
And strangers often at our graves
    Will ask, " What works did they ? "

And every friend that loveth much,
    And every jealous one,
Will give us credit after death
    For only what we've done.

So God in Heaven, when we shall come
    To ask our place therein,
Will judge what heritage to give
    By what our·lives have been.

——§——

EAST OF MOUNT DIABLO.

THE NORTHER.

Steadily, steadily, cold, so cold,
Frosty and sharp, dreary and bold,
    Bloweth the strong north wind,
Down from the.bleak Sierras blown—
Throwing a blight o'er the acres sown,
    Cometh the fiend—north wind.
North wind bold, hold, hold,
    Stay your mighty greed!
Kind of might, blight, blight,
    Follows where you lead.

THE WESTER.

How fast they ride—the clouds!
How swiftly by the white-winged legions fly!
The west wind chills, and rolling o'er the hills
    Thick fog the mountain shrouds.

The sun his glory hides;
The fields look dark; no more the song of lark
Strikes merry notes; long ranks of nimbus float
    Along the low hill-sides.

The creaking shutters mourn;
The windmill whirls convulsively; there curls
Blue smoke about the eaves, until it leaves
    In air, wind-tossed and torn.

FROM THE SOUTH.

There's a warmer touch upon my hand;
    There's a kiss on my mouth,
    From the heart of the South;
'Tis the dewy breath of another land.

There's a trailing mist along the lane;
    There's a vow and a sigh
    From the East born anigh,
'Tis the vow and the sigh of the rain.

———

Hark! how against the panes
The great drops dash! Now quickly raise the sash,

And hear how sweet the murmuring sounds we greet,
For *now*, thank God, *it rains.*

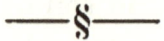

LIKE THE RAIN.

LIKE an arm around me thrown,
As I, fainting, fall alone;
Like a joyful message sent
When the soul with grief is spent;
Like the grasp of friendly hand
In some lonely foreign land;
Like to any sweet surprise,
Bringing gladder destinies,
Is the sudden fall of rain
On the parched and suffering grain.

Like the kiss of peace between
Them who bitterness have seen;
Like the swift-returning breath
Of a dear one saved from death;
Like the glory that will come
After victory has been won;
Like the lifting of the soul,
When the burdens from it roll,
Is the growing of the grain
After God's abundant rain.

HAND IN HAND WITH SORROW.

O FRIENDS, so careless do we go,
    So heedless of the morrow,
That every one of ye, I wist,
    Go hand in hand with sorrow.

Oh, list ye, how the papers read!
    A heart goes homeward singing,
But from the threshold wounded sore
    The dove of peace goes winging.

Another Eve leaves Paradise
    To taste forbidden pleasure.
Ah! will not pain be weighed to her
    With measure unto measure?

A man who in the pride of life
    To justice gave no heeding,
Falls by a brother's wrathful hand,
    His heart's blood swiftly bleeding.

We are too heedless of our lives
    And all their grave transactions;
Too oft the fevered dreams we live
    Give way to sad reactions.

We fail to garner all-year friends
    While shines the sky above us;

And lo! when crushing storms sweep down
  We have no friends to love us.

Oh! strive, dear friends, lest we should fail,
  More earnestness to borrow;
Be *humble, lest ye unawares*
  Walk hand in hand with sorrow.

—§—

A LITTLE LOVING WOMAN.

Now, who will come when I am faint,
  With death's approach above me,
To hold my hand and smooth my brow,
  And cheer the ones who love me?

And who will stand beside my bed,
  The while her heart is breaking,
And say with loving words to them,
  "'Tis best she is not waking."

And who will place white flowers about,
  To make the sad house brighter,
And serve with gentle step and hand
  That sorrow's gloom be lighter.

I know right well she is the one
  Who comes the last with praising

Who most for earth's sad suffering ones
   Her helpful voice is raising.

You know her well.   Oh, every one
   Has such a friend so human,
A noon-tide friend, a night-time friend,
   A li tle loving woman.

———§- —-

A LESSON OF TRUST.

THE morning dawns so radiant, sweet, and clear
No one would think the night had been so drear,
A night of wakefulness and fitful sleep,
When loud-voiced clocks the long-drawn vigils keep;
A night of restlessness to young and old,
A night of sudden sounds and gusts of cold,
And wailing winds creaking about the caves,—
Such night as in its empty darkness grieves
For the sad earth within its silent fold:
Earth many sorrows to the night has told.

But now I wake; the morn is calm and still,
The sunshine smiling on the window-sill;
The birds float singing on the quiet air,
The morning joys to find itself so fair.
I rise ashamed of all the night's unrest.
Even so, when sorrow fills the trembling breast,
Forbear with doubt and pain the hours to spend,
But, trusting God, wait calmly to the end.

GOLDEN DAYS.

THESE are golden days,
  And all the yellow distance of the plain
Has veiled beneath a low-hung, purple haze
  The glory of its grain.

Summer's calm delight
  Waves tremulous along the distant hill,
Comes gleaming down the stream, and flecks with light
  The shadows wide and still.

Low is the chant of day;
  Time passes on unmindful of its hours,
And spring's exultant song has followed away
  The gay and changeful flowers.

The rain-hung zephyrs wait
  While the ripe grain is gathered in its gold;
The weary vine lays down its wealth of grapes,
  And summer weareth old.

Rest is in the air;
  Man gathers from the earth his just increase,
And soon shall hush the sounds of hurrying care
  Beneath God's ordered peace.

The harvest moon is bright;
  And when the brilliant day wears gray and old,
The waiting radiance showers all the night
  With silver for the gold.

THE OAKS OF TULARE.

Go up the broad valley, the far land, the fair land,
  Where the plain stretches on like a slumbering sea,
Where rivers flow down from high mountains snow-
      crowned,
 · And the wind seeks the desert to roam and be free.
Go there when sweet April her soft showers carry
To the wonderful grove land, the oaks of Tulare.

Go there in bright June when the slow-creeping
      shadows,
  In the rank meadow grasses lie dewy and cool;
The boughs all attune with the sky-larks and linnets,
  While the soft winds of summer the leafy courts
      rule.
One still autumn day in thy green aisles to tarry
Is forever to love thee, dear oaks of Tulare.

I see the blue sky and the high fretted arches,
  And the moss-tangled branches all knotted and gray;
Fond memory pictures the calm, sacred places
  Where I waited and loitered that happy June day.
While Hope, eager-winged as some comforting fairy,
Is alluring me back to the oaks of Tulare.

Great oaks, leading up to the steep, sunny hill-sides,
  Stretching down to the banks of the slow, winding
    stream,

I see through thy vistas the homestead, the cottage,
  And the pink-tinted orchards in radiance gleam.
Some day may I rest there, long, glad years to tarry,
In my wonderful grove land, the oaks of Tulare.

——§——

THE QUEEN.

IMPASSIONED day has gone,
    And night serene
Her star-bright robe assumes in soft array,
    And sits a queen,
On high, lone hills uplifted far away.

——§——

NONCHALANCE.

OWLET, nodding thus so quaintly
While the first pale star gleams faintly ·
    From the purple sky,
Pray, what think you of my roaming,
As I pass you in the gloaming,
    Going slowly by?

I would know what you are thinking
With your wide-eyed, steady blinking,
    And your solemn bow.

You have guessed my secret surely,
Looking sidewise so demurely.
  Ah, I wonder how!

I had thought that none would see me,
As I walked out here to free me
  From the parlor's glare;
For I love the gray night falling,
And the noise of crickets calling
  From the stubble there.

I have felt subdued and routed,
I have felt my courage scouted,
  By the wicked day.
'Twas for solitude and grieving,
And to meet the wide, cool evening
  That I came this way.

But you sat up there to meet me,
And kept bowing thus to greet me,
  Looking grave and wise.
I've no doubt you have a heart in
All this gloom and dusk, and darkening
  Of the summer skies.

And your air is so supremely
Quaint and odd, with no unseemly
  Look of outward pain,
I must thank you, owlet, surely;
I'll just bow, like you, demurely,
  If chagrined again.

A FIELD LESSON.

THE fields are ripe for the cutting,
  Growing since early spring,
While we to the summer's fullness
  No gifts of toil can bring.

The sickle will come in gladness,
  Felling the rich, ripe grain,
While lives go out unfruitful,
  In doubting, fear, and pain.

The earth yields up to its Maker—
  Lo! at his bidding stands
Ready and ripe with its fruitage
  Gathered by needy hands.

No doubt takes hold of the river;
  No scoffing stops the shower;
No unbelief in its fetters
  Takes from the seed its power.

The wind comes up from the South land,
  Asking not whence it blows;
There falls tree seed, unerring,
  From each wild wind that blows.

O souls that bow unto nature,
  Loving her wondrous ways,

Learn from her workings, duty;
    Take up her songs of praise.

Praise God in his creations,
    Nor doubt your years away,
Lest the fruits of your life be lacking
    On God's great harvest-day.

—§—

HERE LIES AN HONEST MAN.

" ONE dearly loved lies here,"
    They say with grief,
Who knew without a doubt or fear
    His heart's belief.

One noble, generous, true,
    So say his peers;
" He builded better than he knew "
    These quiet years.

" Here lies an honest man,"
    Cry all the town,
Who made his nobleness a ban
    To keep him down.

Who loved men's eyes to blind,
    Were not with him;

His shining soul the world unkind
Could not bedim.

Beside his grave they bow
Who once gave hate;
They cannot vilify him now;
His fame is great.

" Here lies an honest man,"
So say we all.
Command a kinglier praise who can !
This covers all.

———§———

THE SUPREME THOUGHT.

At morn when the air is fragrant,
At noon when the heat is high,
At night when the starry wonders
Mount to the solemn sky;
At morn when my faith is strongest,
At noon when my hope is clear,
At night when my heart is trembling
Under its load of fear,
Thoughts of such beautiful presence
Are guarding my joy and pain,
" That I wait for their welcome coming
As flowers await the rain."

And the thought that makes all thinking
    The thought that is all in all,
Is the thought that all creation
    Under God's eye doth fall.
· The earth in his hand he holdeth,
    And space he filleth afar
With systems of suns that sparkle,
    Star unto gliding star.

He teaches the laws to fear him,
    He marks the progress of time,
He gives to the comet its ages
    To go on its pathway sublime,
He teaches the birds their singing,
    He writeth his name on high,
And paints on the roadside blossom
    The hue of the summer sky.

And this is the thought that cheereth,
    The thought that is all in all:
Though crowns and kingdoms shall tremble,
    His promise will never fall.
And though it is fear and darkness,
    And though it is warmth and light,
His limitless power is keeping
    Each child of his love in sight.

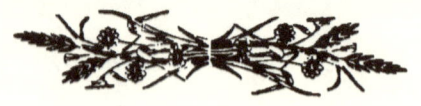

IN MEMORIAM.

SALLIE WYTHE WILLIAMS.

GOD loved her so—ah! well,
Sweet soul, farewell
We would not say
To any love of God: nay, nay.

We would not stay the love
That draws above
Those honored best,
Elect to shine upon his breast.

God needed her. 'Tis well;
Dear heart, farewell!
Full well we know
Redeeming love has willed it so.

We needed her. 'Tis best
God gives *her* rest,
And gives to *earth*
The dower of her perfect worth.

God loved her most: Amen!
Take comfort then,
Sad, stricken home:
Her soul triumphant seeks its own.

CARRIE CLIFFORD WENK.

[From " Life's Highway," an Alumni poem.]

AND the years bear us on.   There's a message
  My heart would deliver to-night,
From a soul that has passed from the highway
  To the beautiful city of light.
How soon on the heavenly records
  The sum of her duty was told,
The first through our gateway of garlands,
  The first through the gateway of gold.

Dear, dutiful toiler!   Dear sister of light!
  Thy name and thy memory sweet
Shall be unto me on the highway of life
  A light and a guide to my feet.
And out of the brightness she leaneth to-night,
  Her soul's admonition I hear.
O wandering spirits of earth! life is short;
  Be ready, lest He shall appear.

——§——

RUBY RICHARDSON.

[Died at Byron, 1887, aged two years and eight months.]

BACK, back, cruel fears!
  Cease, cease, blinding tears,
Nor flow till the soul is asunder!

Her eyes drooping low,
Her breath coming slow,—
Does God call her homeward, I wonder?

Hush, hush, bleeding hearts!
The life tendril parts;
Hope bursts from our clinging embraces;
And down through the skies
A bright legion flies,
Swift winging from God's holy places.

No, no, waiting host;
We love her the most;
Come take from our midst any other.
God's mercy seems cold
That enwrapped us of old.
Has God ceased to pity, sad mother?

See, see, at the throne
Christ standeth alone,
The child on his bosom enfolden!
While, lo! on her brow,
So glorified now,
The gleam of a star is beholden.

Yes, yes; God is wise;
He knows we will rise
By the strength of the love that is round her.
And so for the work
Her child spirit wrought
Already the Father has crowned her.

Child Ruby is dead;
Her child spirit, wed
To the hopes of the kingdom immortal,
Will patiently wait,
And watch at the gate
For the dear ones who drift to the portal.

——§——

CHILD ARMS.

[During my short experience in teaching, no pupils were so endeared
to me as those of my primary class in Dixon, Solano County. In the
autumn of 1876, that town was visited by diphtheria in its most fatal
form, and many of the school children were its victims. There is no
lament that will give any conception of the sorrow of the stricken town.
The following amateur lines were written the succeeding spring, and
are presented, by request, without change or revision.]

DEAR little child arms, come gather about me;
    Come with the "warmth of your loving embrace;"
Fling off the shadows that darken upon me;
    Lay thy soft touches again on my face.

Dear little child arms, so gentle and loving,
    Warmed by child hearts that trusted me so,
Come in your whiteness and eager caressing,
    Rescue my heart from its breaking and woe.

Loving, white child arms, I call for you vainly;
    Sorrow has covered my life with its wave;
Over the hills where the sunset is golden,
    Child arms are folded and cold in the grave.

Precious child arms, that have strengthened me often,
    Do you not long for my sorrow to cease ?
Come from your silence so long and so dreary,
    Lighten my heart with your touches of peace.

Dear little child arms were glad in the spring-time,
    Tossing the blossoms they gave for my love;
Blossoms have withered, and sere leaves have fallen,
    Child arms are bearing the wreaths up above.

Long is the life the Death Angel has left us,
    Weary the world with its changes and pain,
Up in a haven of glory and gladness,
    Child arms are waiting to clasp me again.

—§—

ON THE DEATH OF GERTRUDE WELLING-TON.

[Preceptress of Napa Collegiate Institute.]

SHINING angels, were you lonely
That you came and took her only
    Whom we loved ?
Did you need another glory
Bearing on the old, old story,
    Up above?

Did your shining ranks lack brightness,
That you snatched the only whiteness
    On the earth ?

As you bore her onward sweeping,
Were you sad to leave us weeping
    .   For her worth?

Ah! I ween the hosts came thronging,
When the spirits brought the dawning
        Of her soul!
And they touched the gold harps lightly.
As her glowing feet sped brightly
        To their goal.

Crowning angels, cease your speaking,
For your brightest crown, go seeking
        For her head.
Oh, the glowing stars there burning,
Of her pure and patient earning!
        Blessed dead!

Friend, disciple, faithful teacher,—
All our sighing cannot reach her,
        Loved and best.
Think, O bursting hearts that weep her,
Should our selfish wishes keep her
        From her rest?

Bless the kind eyes, dropped so meekly!
Bless the dear heart loved so deeply,
        Strong in prayer.
Meet us on the pearly portal,
Greet us on the streets immortal
        Over there.

 # MOODS.

MY HANDS.

WHAT if the fickle world go slow
   And merit wear poor raiment?
What if the noble deeds men do,
   Have no reward or payment?
What if the royal road to wealth
   Has ways of strange contortion?
Distrust and fear clog not my soul;
   These hands will earn my portion.

These hands can earn my honest bread,
   Without a friend or favor;
And little cares this trusty arm
   When weak-souled flatterers waver;
The world may spurn me if it will,
   And all my great endeavor;
But still my soul walks proud and strong,
   And these brave hands toil ever.

I fear not labor and its ways,
   No earthen chain can bind me;
In lethargy of slow content,
   No needful day will find me.
There is a time of patient trust,
   A time for sudden springing,
And while I wait the hour of fate,
   I bless what toil is bringing.

Meanwhile, if sudden turns the wheel,
　And brings me sweet promotion,
From wealth and honor, fame and friends,
　I'll claim my just proportion.
But then what things are pure and true.
　God every day is giving;
And while my life goes calmly on
　These hands will earn my living.

——§——

A WALK.

Let me alone to walk:
I want to see God, and talk
With the dun cloud moving high,
With the field-lark darting by,
With the myriad things in the grain
That wake and live since the rain;
The flowers will come and talk:
Leave me alone to walk.

No, it is not too far,
Where a thousand fancies are,
Born of the motion and life,
Of the flowers and grass in strife
With the buffeting wind.   Thought
With each vigorous step is inwrought.
The winds God's messengers are:
No, it is not too far.

Leave me alone to walk:
Unkind you were, in your talk,
To charge me with evil design,
To charge me with thought malign.
Life is as frail as a flower
Born in a windy hour:
Why should we slander and mock?
Leave me alone to walk.

But it is ever so:
Not the heart's best grace we know
But what we judge to be
From what we are blind to see.
We are seeing the rough, hard bur,
Not the soul within astir.
So, pardon my deeds in your talk,
But leave me alone to walk.

——§——

THE CALIFORNIA LITERARY AND SCIENTIFIC CIRCLE.

LISTEN! did you hear the flowing
Of a streamlet gently going,
    Flowing through our thirsty land?
How it seeks its winding courses,
From its far-off coastland sources,
    Urged by some divine command!

O Chautauqua! Holy mother!
Flows this stream as flows no other,
    From thy consecrated heart.
We will press to meet it yearning;
O thou stream of Christian learning,
    Permeate our every part!

How we need thee, happy river!
In thy flowing, flow on ever;
    Flood us with thy waves divine.
Lave us in thy wondrous coolness,
Source of every earthly fullness:
    Wisdom, wisdom, be it mine.

Mark you, there will come the dawning
Of a rare and fruitful morning,
    All our humble lives among;
Patient lives will grow more saintly,
Fires of evil glow more faintly,
    Hearts once silent find a tongue.

Flowers will spring o'er pathways lonely,
Brought and watered by thee, only,
    Christian flood of life and light;
And the children wandering sadly
Through their barren youth will gladly
    Tarry where thy stream is bright.

And from all our door-steps lowly
We may see the visions holy

That we never hoped to find,—
Visions of the sunlit mountains,
Visions of the tireless fountains,
   That are in the land of mind.

Every science leads us to Him,
Every art its pathway through Him;
   History writes the name of God.
And this stream in channels earthward,
Going on will bear us worthward,
   Upward, upward from the sod.

While the Father, looking kindly
On his subjects, who so blindly
   Wander in the ways of sin,
Guards this stream in all its highways,
Guides it through its many byways,
   Guides it purified to Him.

—§—

A REGAL LIFE.

I WOULD that I were brave
To do aright life's little deeds,
That no one ever notes or heeds,
   But seem to us so grave;

Were brave enough to take
A portion of my speeding hours,
A bounty from my thoughts and powers
　　To spend for others' sake.

I would that I were strong,
To say to my own voice, Be still,
Else speak no careless word to chill
　　Some better heart with wrong.

And I would sit with pride;
Or else deceit will take her place
To throw a curtain o'er my face
　　I cannot draw aside.

I would that I might reign;
Might rule the kingdom of my heart,
That not an evil thought could start,
　　To scatter words of pain.

And I would wear a crown;
Yet take from none such beauteous right;
Its jewels would be virtues bright,
　　Humility my gown.

For friends who with me stand
I'd have the noblest of my race;
Who'd scorn to turn a changeful face
　　Or give a traitorous hand.

A courtly peace I'd see,
To leave no gentle deed undone,
Nor hatred feel from anyone,—
Life's splendid equity.

——§——

PRESCIENCE.

I WOKE one morn with hope upon my heart,
Borne inward by some influence yet unknown;
Warm strength unloosed sped outward to my hands,
And evil doubt seemed moved and overthrown.

Dark, brooding phantoms from my soul had fled,
And far-faint voices softly moved to sing;
A love long stilled set pallid cheeks all red,
And then I knew, nor looked abroad, *'twas Spring.*

——§——

THE PASSING OF SPRING.

UNDERNEATH the dew, damp grasses,
Winter grasses rank and cold,
Lies the soul of spring-time sleeping,
Breathing lightly through the mould.

When, erelong, the West Wind passes
With a love-song ages old,

And the starry flowers leaping,
  Have her earth-born passion told,

She will wake and stir the grasses,
  Wear her vesture so unrolled,
Till the love-light in her keeping
  Touches all the green with gold.

—§—

REPININGS.

THERE is a loneliness in life
  No human love can sever;
Though arm is linked to loving arm,
  Thought walks alone forever.

There is a path that each must tread
  Untrod by any other;
The slender thread each walking weaves,
  Fate cannot join together.

The thoughts that rise to touch the heart,
  To make it sighs or singing,
Come on their own swift pinions spread,
  Life's lonely pathways winging.

We look in the loving eyes that shine,
  Unspoken things discerning,
And wonder then if look meets look
  With yearning unto yearning.

About our hearts cold mists lie close
    Like peaks in cloudy weather,
And souls unknown, unloved, unfelt,
    Walk life's long path together.

O faith in death! O sweet beyond!
    O life of new divining!
How bright thy gleamings shine afar,
    To check this earth's repining!

—§—

THE KNIGHT OF THE NINETEENTH CENTURY.

TO THOMAS STEVENS.

SIR STEVENS of the wheel!
Thy valorous deeds will wake the ancient lyre,
Ten thousand maiden hearts to love inspire,
    Who, dreaming day and night,
    Will see the silver light,
Streaming in danger lands behind thy tire!

Knight of the wingéd steed!
Dear to thy native land are all thy deeds;
And yet most dear that high and noble creed
    That spurns the burning cup.
    How art thou lifted up,
With golden shield like *that* to serve thy need!

7

God speed thee, noble knight!
I pray thy safe return from wild, weird lands ;
From cold, grim mountains and the desert sands.
  Calm is the Golden Gate,
  Where we thy entrance wait,
To deck thy steed and thee with medal bands.

——§——

AGE AND LOVE.

——

Age tarries not for beauty;
No favors doth he seek;
  But drawing near
  Each hurrying year
He snatches roses from thy fair, fair cheek.

He heedeth not my speaking,
Nor counsels with my dread;
  I fear to name
  His fateful claim,
Or see his touches on thy gold-bright head.

But all is well, O fond heart!
Love keepeth equal pace,
  And through thy tears
  And through my fears
He holds his kisses to thy pale, pale face.

SOLITUDE.

AND now, my soul, shut out the worldly smile,
    The bold, rude laughter,
    And sly mocking after,
While we with solitude commune a while.

And in this cloister, free from cruel eyes,
    For long redression,
    We will make confession
Before life's holy Priest of sacrifice.

O kind, best Comforter, my Priest and King,
    Before thee, kneeling,
    I disguise no feeling;
My weakness, pain, humility, I bring.

Make penitence, my soul, thy need is great.
    Thy strength is weakness,
    Thy assurance, meekness,
Unto the struggles that before thee wait.

And, yea, make penitence, O heart of mine,
    Confess thy yearning
    For those great lights burning,
Those stars that cannot on thy pale life shine.

Dear Heart of solitude, I cling to thee;
    Such warm peace folds me,
    Such calm strength upholds me,
A gift of power groweth inwardly.

My soul no longer sinks beneath its pain;
　　The silences grow dearer,
　　And glimmering nearer,
The long, long hopes of life shine out again.

And every olden love that lingers yet,
　　With sweet intrusion,
　　On my soul's seclusion,
Comes softly in to bid me not forget.

The benediction falls, I go my way;
　　And, musing slowly,
　　From the cloister holy
I walk the aisles that lead to working day.

——§——

MY FAITH.

I HAVE such faith in life
That I could walk a bleak and barren hill,
And meadow songs the silent air would fill,
Through my imagining and high desire
To keep heart strong, although my feet may tire.
I have such faith that autumn shall be spring,
If I would have it so, and beauty cling
To leafless tree or barren wind-swept field.
A painted blossom will old fragrance yield,
And by my faith a pictured face will speak,
And bring warm blushes to my pallid cheek.

I have such faith in death
That I could leave life's promises that wait,
And pass with heart expectant through the gate.
Faith is not faith, my soul, love is not love,
If founded not on faith in God above.
What earnestness I have, what powers I keep,
Would not lie breathless with my body's sleep;
Each pale, uncurtained star that shines for me
Will dawn resplendent in eternity;
And love with me shall rise, when fails this breath,
To some high Heaven—such is my faith in death.

—§—

WINDOW PLANTS.

My window plants turn to the sun,
Reaching out every one
For the smiles of the great gold face
Thrown down through the limited space.

The sun, with its marvelous grace,
Wins back to its face
Each branch that I freedom denied,
And turned to the room inside.

And the rose geranium, pride
Of them all, at its side,
Holds high with long stems, to the noon,
Its many-leaved clusters of bloom.

Turning its beautiful rose-hued bloom
Away from the low, dark room,
To the strengthening, beautiful one,
The joy of the morning, the sun.

So is love to the heart, the sun,
Great, glorious one !
Leading up and out of the night
Life's passionate blossoms of light.

PEACE.

I FEEL the tide of life sweep on;
I see the days die one by one;
Youth takes his garlands and is gone,
    And yet I am content.

I see toil fling its hope away,
And life becomes a working day,
Where courage has no power to stay,
    And yet I keep my peace.

I see the triumphs I would wear
Like falling stars fade into air,
Beyond the reach of toil or prayer,
    Yet still I am content.

I thought to gather gorgeous flowers
To glorify my rainy hours;

Alas! they lose their gladdening powers,
  For all I miss them not.

I see the heights where I would stand,
To view the vales of Beulah land,
By dim, immeasurable distance spanned,
  And yet I weary not.

It is so sweet to live with all,
Though tears upon our failures fall;
High hopes and triumphs are not all,
  There is no joy but peace.

'Tis toiling for the after rest,
'Tis deeming present joy the best,
'Tis finding each day fair and blest,
  That maketh me content.

MY FATHER'S HOUSE.

As I toil for life's treasures and blessings,
  And am fainting of labor and zest,
Oh, how sweet it is sometimes to tarry
  At the house of my father to rest!

To forget for the time what my care is,
  To abandon my struggle and pain;

And to sleep 'neath the roof of my father,
   While I dream of my childhood again!

What a feeling of safety comes o'er me,
   As father is locking the door!
And the clock he is winding so calmly
   Is the trusted time-keeper of yore.

It is value to value—the world's way—
   And you take what your merits receive;
And no comrades or friends give the welcome
   That our fathers and mothers can give,—

While each chair, and each couch, and each comfort
   Seem to add to your welcome complete,
And you fancy that all things are striving
   To rejoice with your home-coming feet.

Oh, the fathomless love of the home folks!
   It restrains us wherever we roam,
And no time or condition can shadow
   The return of the wanderer home.

And I think, when life's path grows a-weary,
   And the dews of the night on me lie,
I should like to be borne through the gloaming
   To the house of my father to die.

THEN.

[On reading " Untimely Thoughts," by T. B. Aldrich.]

SHRINKING at the thought of death, dear?
Grown sad in this comfort and cheer?
As if death were something to fear?

Why, *then* 'twill be dark like the night;
These gleams will have faded out quite;
You'll pine like a child for the light.

The morn will be gone with its bloom;
Forgotten the triumphs of noon;
Night comes to the worn none too soon.

What seemeth so fair now and sweet
Will be to your heart's failing beat
Too old, like a dream to repeat.

Your life like the seeds will be old;
From the dead, dried limb to the mould
You will fall, not fearing the cold.

You'll be freeing your soul, then, of sod;
You'll be nearing the pathway untrod;
You'll be reaching your hands up to God.

We'll be *glad*, it seems to me, dear,
And welcome the rest of the bier,
No matter what day or what year.

A PERFECT LIFE.

A CHILDHOOD unknowing sorrow,
    Unfettered by creed and rule;
Of frolic and mirth and flowers
    A childish measure full.

A youth with a mother's blessing,
    Making it glad and sweet,
And the zest of a new ambition
    To hasten the lagging feet.

A strength'ning of will and purpose,
    A walking from sin apart,
And finding that toil supplieth
    The wants of the hand and heart.

A summer of life grown tranquil,
    A finding of love's desire,
A gathering of friends and children
    Unto the household fire.

A keeping of hope untarnished,
    A walking in humble ways,
And leaving the heights of glory
    To the light of Heaven's days.

A coming of deep contentment,
    And cherishing first and best

The strong, calm trust in duty
   That keepeth the heart at rest.

The speeding of autumn gently,
   With never a thought of tears;
A giving to God's most needy
   Thanks for the fruitful years.

A welcome of snow soft falling,
   With a snow-white heart within;
And a winter warmed and sheltered
   By the love of kith and kin.

—§—

TO ONE, A POET.

WRITE me a poem, sweet friend, new friend,
   Just as you'd write to one
Known to be helpless and frail and weak,
   Fearing the noonday sun.

You are so fearless and strong, sweet friend,
   True to your shining way,
With truth for the true, love for the fair,
   And songs for the cloudy day.

Your way has no turning to doubt and grief;
   Firm are your passing feet

As you climb with flinging of flowers away,
   The blossoming heights you seek.

Write me a poem, brave friend, true friend,
   Tuned with the love you bear
To those who falter, finding with pain
   Only the weeds of care.

Make it a frame-work of faith, dear friend,
   Faith of the praying heart;
Haply some strength on its verses borne
   May to my spirit start.

Make it all shining with hope, fair hope,
   Sprung from a heart of toil;
Haply a gleam of your lighted lamp
   Onto my path may fall.

Write it in charity, friend, new friend,
   Born of all human needs;
Give it with love of thy poet's heart,
   Sweetest of all thy creeds.

—§—

COMPANIONSHIP.

TO MARY TRACY MOTT.

A STAR shot out of heaven, I say,
   When one above, apart,

Came near to me
So I could see
The beating of her heart.

A star shot out of heaven to-day;
I walked the earth alone,
When she to me
Dropped sympathy,
From near a shining throne.

A star not lost or cast away;
She none the less is bright
For stooping so
To me below,
All trembling for her light.

A star came down to me, I say;
For so, indeed, it seemed,
That she, a friend,
Should kindness lend,
Of which I once but dreamed.

——§——

PRESSED VIOLETS IN A BORROWED CLASSIC.

Wise "old heathen" who were living
Twenty centuries ago,
What aromas sweetly modern
From your tedious pages flow!

Breath of violets, strangely mingled
  With Demosthenes and Greece;
Arts of war and laws Platonic,
  Hiding these shy arts of peace.

Friend, I see you, absent-minded,
  Turning these wise pages o'er,
Leaving here for safer keeping
  Those sweet flowers that she wore.

None would search here, you were thinking,
  Or would seeing understand,
How she gave them you, half jesting,
  With a pressure of the hand.

Friend, I think these old lawgivers
  Far too ponderous for my mind;
Thanks for leaving, absent-minded,
  Something I could read, if blind.

I have pondered truly, deeply,
  What the wise and ancient say,
But the truest thing I read here
  Is a tale of yesterday.

THE MONTHLY MAGAZINE.

GOOD friend! Good friend! Oh, faithful more than all!
    Oh, wise and rich-voiced guest,
    Kind champion of rest,
Thrice welcome when the evening shadows fall !

Days may be dark, and nights be lacking cheer,
    While sullen rain-clouds beat
    The garden path and street;
But all is well, warm friend, when thou art near.

Oh, faithful more than all! *They* are not so;
    A little heat or cold,
    A little thought half-told,
And they who seemed the dearest turn and go.

Foes have not turned thee from my lonely door.
    Through slanderous darts unkind,
    My portals still you find,
Not less to love me, but to serve me more.

Thou dost for me a hundred heartaches keep,
    Which, told to other friends,
    Would serve unseemly ends,
To turn again and rend me ere I sleep.

Thou canst all places and all seasons bless.
    E'en to the couch of pain
    Thou dost admittance gain,
Offering bright fancies to forgetfulness.

Most courteous guest, oh, welcome more than all !
    Wise watcher of my care,
    Prince of the study chair,
Thrice welcome when the evening shadows fall !

CUPID CLIPPED.

Poor love, he wasn't quite resigned
    To like our humb'e ways,
On cottage faith and cottage fare
    To spend his golden days.
He liked not well the daily toil,
    He magnified our needs,
And made me wear uneasy care
    By his capricious deeds.

Poor little, willful, wingéd boy!
    He longed for ease and art,
And shot, unseen, ambitions keen
    To lacerate my heart.
He begged for jewels numberless,
    Soft luxuries a host,
And put to flight both day and night
    The peace I treasured most.

He poised before the open door,
    He fluttered at the pane,
As if to try the windy sky
    And ne'er come back again.
He saw the crimson clouds above,
    He spurned my offerings;
What could I do?   His flight I'd rue,
    And so I clipped his wings.

He must not sigh, dear, foolish boy,
  For bric-a-brac and toys;
Nor let a prayer for paintings rare
  Destroy our cottage joys.
He must descend to lowly wants
  And common work-day things.
For fancies spent and discontent,
  Poor boy! I clipped his wings.

And now he seemeth quite content
  To brew the foaming yeast;
To knead and bake, and strive to make
  Each homely meal a feast.
He sweeps the room with loving will,
  To keep it warm and bright,
And cottage chairs and cottage wares
  Are bathed in rosy light.

'Tis better so; for drear indeed
  The cottage hall would be
If love were sped and beauty fled
  From life's simplicity.
Low life can be both grand and good,
  And cottagers be kings,
Though oft we must to keep our trust,
  Sweet Cupid, clip his wings.

8

THE NEED.

I LOVE the cold, strong air,
The rain on my face and hair,
For my cheeks well need, you see,
The roses they leave with me.

I say that I do not mind
The word and reproof unkind
If they teach me better things
Than my vain imaginings.

—§—

HIGH NOON.

WHAT if thy life,
Now coming to its prime,
  Should gladden in its strength,
    And prove more rich and sweet
Than all youth's promise-time!
    What if high noon,
With light serene and fine,
  Should glorify life's length,
    And show thee made complete:
Life's best in its decline.

NAY, NOT WIND.

Baby died long ago,
Ere life's star went sinking low.

Then love's gladness made me strong,
Made my life a morning song.

He, my king, my trust, my pride,
Led me, clinging, glorified.

But all that has faded slow,
All the anguish and the woe;

And she is dead, whose form and face
Lured him from my plainer grace.

My wifehood spurned, love turned to hate,
And my life grew desolate,

As the winter fields of snow;
But all that was long ago.

No, no, friend, there is no pain,
As I breathe these airs again.

What was that upon my lips?
At my throat light finger-tips!

Something on my cold cheek pressed,
Something lay upon my breast!

Nay, '*twas not* the warm sunshine
Thrilling to my heart like wine.

Nay, 'twas *not* the west wind's pace;
Silken ringlets touched my face;

Silken ringlets, soft and fair,
Touched me in the empty air.

On the west wind from the plain,
Came my baby's arms again!

Ah, these hot, impetuous tears!
Such I have not shed for years.

Naught on earth could move me so:
Baby died long ago.

PLOWING UNDER THE FLOWERS.

PLOUGHING under the flowers,
   Wet by the midnight showers,
Turning them over and under,
   My beautiful, beautiful flowers.

Every bright face turned over,
   Smiling down in the clover;

Feet of the horses and plowman
　　First crushing and trampling them over.

Cream and crimson and yellow,
　　Into the furrow mellow,
Covered with clods damp and broken,—
　　Sweet crimson and purple and yellow.

Witness the death of the flowers,
　　Giving the earth new powers;
Sacrificed, slain for their country,
　　My beautiful, beautiful flowers.

—§—

A DROP OF FAITH.

I KNEW the blessed rain was sure to fall,
　　I knew the needy land
　　Was under his command;
I knew the Lord was thinking of us all.

I knew the drying hills would soon be wound
　　By clouds of low-hung mist,
　　And drooping flowers be kissed
By rain-drops pelting to the grateful ground.

I knew the clouds would spread the rich, wide plain,
　　And dripping showers would fall

Where grain grows thick and tall,
And tender stalks would grow for love of rain.

I knew the scraggy oaks, that leaving grow,
      Would shake their new-grown tops,
      And showers of pearly drops
Would glitter on the grassy sward below.

Where rolls such living green the landscape o'er,
      How could we faithless prove!
      God has such boundless love
That where he blesses he will bless the more.

—§—

DARE.

[Read at the Alumni Reunion of Napa College.]

WHAT I speak you have known in your soul:
Through the mists of my thought I have seen
How men rise from the depth, and, supreme,
Walk in glory and peace to their goal.

Walk in glory and peace! They have crossed
The dark valley of fear; they have passed
Through the billows of doubt; at the last
You must cross. You will dare or be lost.

As we labor and do, life is long.
What is fear but a pang, but a wound,
That will spill our heart's blood on the ground?
But to dare is to walk and grow strong.

As we dare we shall climb and grow strong,
And the wind, it shall seem but a song;
And the burdens shall fall, and the lights
Of God's blessing shall shine on the heights.

Not for glory alone should we dare;
There are visions high up in the air;
There are visions of angels and men;
You shall walk with good company then.

You should dare to be purer and higher;
You should dare to look up from the mire;
You should dare to aspire to life's throne
For the grandeur of failure alone.

You will dare to be humble sometime,
In that realm where thought reigneth sublime,
For the truth rises up to the sun;
But humanity grasps, and is done.

What I write you have learned by your years.
You are brave, you are humble, are true,
Then shall life show God's meaning to you,
And great peace shall be measured for tears.

NAPA.

Fair Napa, bowered in
By sweet acacia, made
The trysting place of Spring,
Beloved of sun and shade.

"God's garden" painted there,
A faultless gem thou art!
Pure as a maiden lives
Thy memory in my heart.

— —§— —

THE BEST.

'Twas, after all, the best—
The place of the wild bird's nest,
Built where the bird on the wing
Grew wearied and stopped to sing.

E'en so the heart finds rest;
Troubled and hurt in its quest,
It finds some place by the way
The safest and best to stay.

STRENGTH.

I DARE you to make me sad;
I've found that life is hopeful and fair;
You cannot drag me to any despair,
But some reprieve can be had.

Of my friends there none remain?
The world is wide; there are more to find;
They count but little who stay behind,
If I've not myself to blame.

My name is flung tó the dust?
Then like the flower seed hid from view,
If it cannot rise and blossom anew
'Tis well, and perish it must.

My face as it now appears?
The flower must yield to the fruit.   Far more
Than favors of youth do I hold in store
The wisdom of garnered years.

And love, you can take that too,
But my heart's pure life you cannot take,
Nor the grace it can save for love's sweet sake,
Nor the warmth that will come anew.

'Tis health and zest that are glad?
Then I will be glad till all is lost,
And never despair till the tide is crossed
To the land where none are sad.